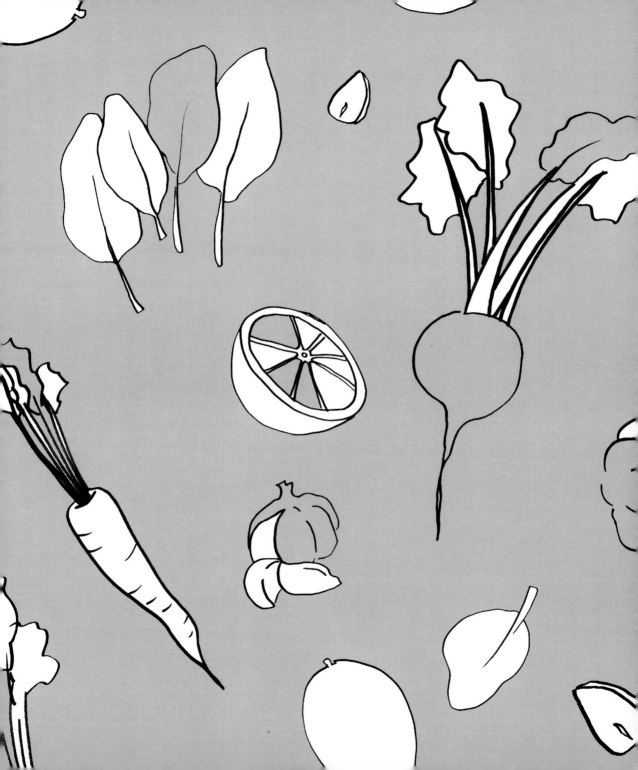

For Ki and Alexander, who are totally pumped;
For my parents, who are compassionate;
For Luke, Lily, Alwyn, Wilder, and all the kids I love!

Manufactured in the United States of America.
Designed by Nathalie VanBalen. Text set in Arial.
ISBN 978-0-578-04136-0
Summary: Two enthusiastic 'vikings' are enthralled with their new juicer and must
decide whether to exploit yellow spotted snails, whose ground-up shells can be used
as a nutrient-rich supplement in juice.
[1.Compassion- fiction. 2.Vegetarianism- fiction. 3.Critical thinking- fiction.]

ThoraThinks Press
4403 A Elkins Avenue
Nashville, TN 37209

www.thorathinks.com

Garlic- Onion- Beet- Spinach- Mango- carrot- Grapefruit Juice

Nathalie VanBalen

ThoraThinks Press
Nashville, Tennessee

Hey there, I'm **Ingvar!**

I assume **you** have **come** here **in search of a story**.

Let me **tell** you about some **friends** of mine—

a family of five who live in this **big**, square-ish house.

hello

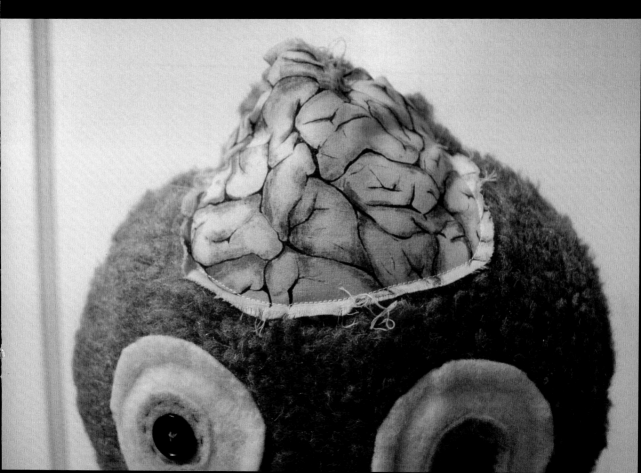

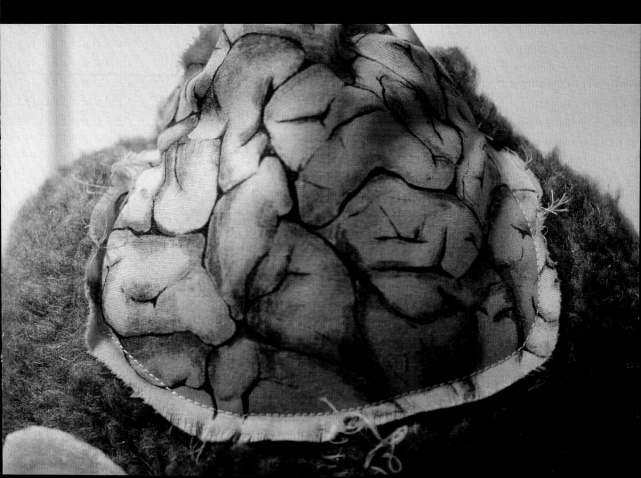

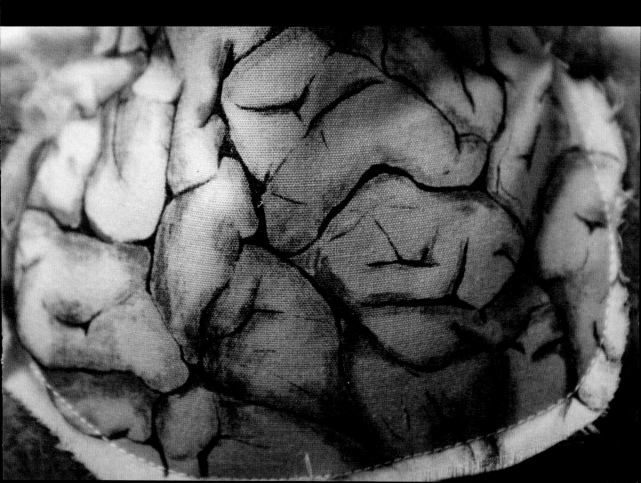

Thora lives with two little tweeters,

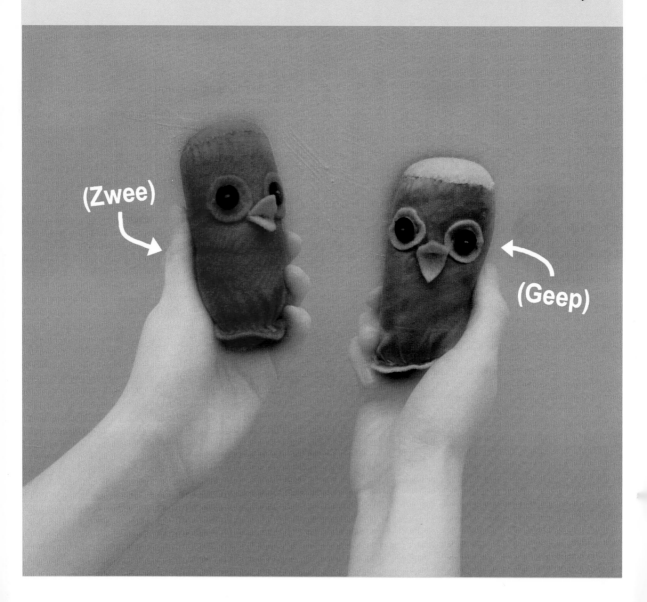

(Zwee)

(Geep)

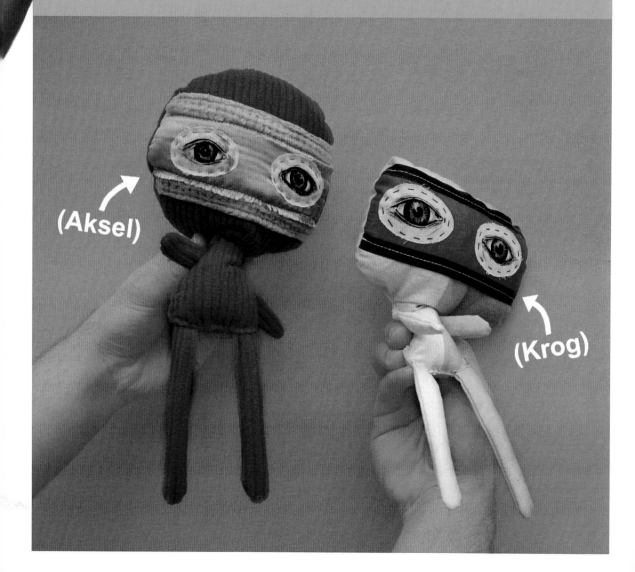

They don't have a ship, they don't go to battle,

and they aren't particularly hairy.

They don't even wear those horn-helmet things.*

*Although, I heard that real vikings hardly ever wear those.

These guys will tell you that they are **TOTALLY** "adventure-oriented."

They're always **pumped** about *something*-

(even about things you wouldn't expect).

They go on **heavy-stuff-adventures:**

Aksel: "**Dude**, let's go pick up heavy stuff!"

Krog: "**Sweet.**"

Aksel: "*Totally* sweet."

green-stuff-adventures:

Krog: "Check it out! I just got **15 bunches** of **kale!**"

Aksel: "Awesome, man. Let's eat **tons** of it!"

Krog: "**Mega-tons.**"

and **loud-stuff-adventures:**

Aksel: "Listen to this **awesome** new metal band I discovered!"

Krog: "They *ARE* awesome! I am **so pumped** now."

Aksel: "I am so **pumped**, too."

Sometimes the vikings get **SO TOTALLY PUMPED**, that they stay up *all night long* blasting music from their stereo and shouting things that don't make much sense at all.

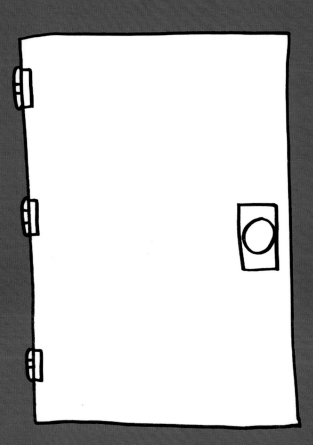

Thora
and the
tweeters
stand by
the door
and listen.

The vikings do sound pretty cute when they're pumped.

But do you know
what gets Aksel
and Krog really,

REALLY,

REA

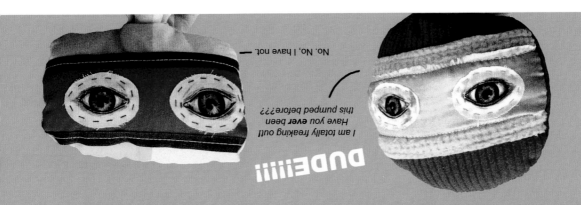

No, No, I have not.

Have you ever been
this pumped before???

I am totally freaking out!

DUDE!!!!!

LLY

pumped???

Ever since they purchased the coveted

Ultra-
Mega-
Super-
Xtreme-
Juicemaster 5000,

they have not been able to stop!

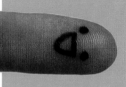

Their current adventure is to juice *EVERYTHING*:

from
cabbages,
cantaloupes,
celery,
and **carrots,**

to
parsnips,
pomegranates,
parsley,
and
pumpkins.

They've tried just about every combination,

but their *FAVORITE* mixture is

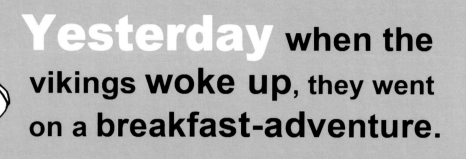

Yesterday when the vikings woke up, they went on a breakfast-adventure.

They made **TONS** of garlic–onion–beet–spinach–mango–carrot–grapefruit juice to share with Thora, Zwee, and Geep.

5000

Everyone gathered around the kitchen table, where they drank their juice and talked about the dreams they'd had during the night.

Some of their **stories** were pretty intense.

So was the juice.

After breakfast,

Adventures of a Bean Girl

Th**o**ra re**a**d **a** funny st**o**ry t**o** the twee**t**er**s**,

while **Aksel and Krog** researched **juicing methods** on the **internet.**

The vikings found a website that got them totally, **TOTALLY** PUMPED.

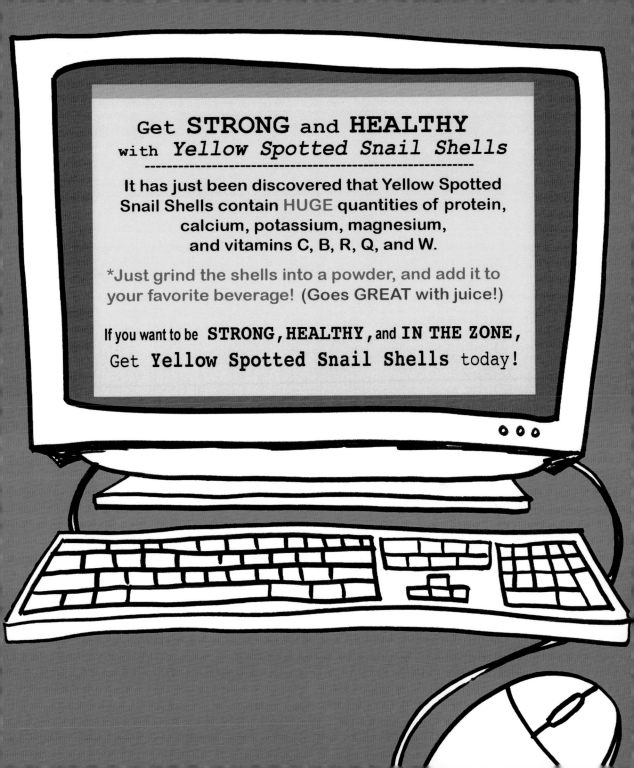

5 nanoseconds later,

Aksel and **Krog** were outside with their snail-catching nets.

They ran around the whole neighborhood, scooping up every single yellow spotted snail they could find.

They absolutely, positively, **COULD NOT WAIT** to make a batch of their *favorite juice* using all the **nutrient-rich snail shells** they had gathered!

Aksel and **Krog** returned
to their big, square-ish house,

carrying nets
FILLED
with yellow spotted snails.

They went
straight
to **the**
kitchen,

and searched
the cabinets
for their
juicer.

Thora heard them bustling around and wanted to see what they were doing.

"Hey vikings! What's going on in here?"

"We are on a **VERY** important juice-adventure," Aksel replied.

"Okay. Well, if you need any help..."

...Thora paused

The vikings explained the situation.

"Thora, their shells are **TOTALLY** nutritious! We're going to **grind them up** and put them **in our juice!**" they said.

_"They will make us incredibly strong and healthy."

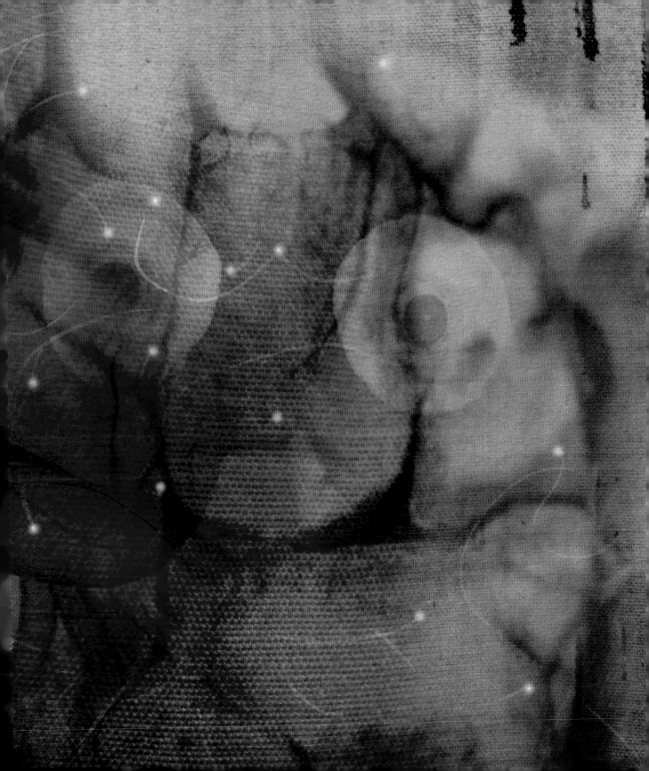

Thora grimaced.

"Yellow spotted snail shells are **not** for vikings," she said, firmly.

"They belong to *yellow spotted snails.*"

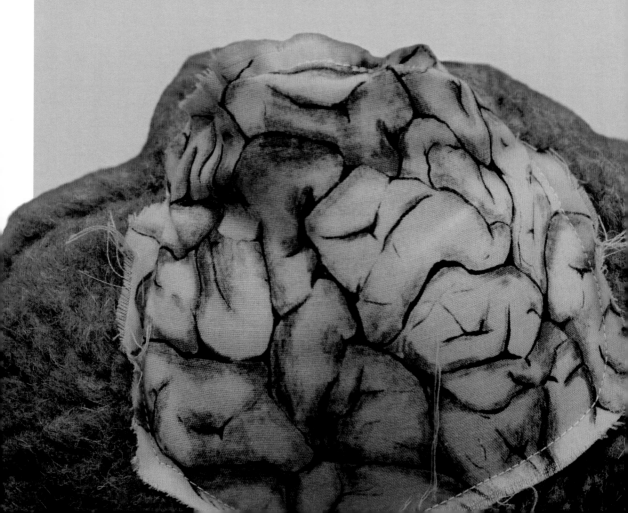

She thought about how the snails were feeling.

What **had they** been **doing** before
the **vikings scooped** them up?

Maybe they were **playing** with their **snail friends**.
Maybe they were **taking care** of their **snail** babies.
Maybe **they were** nibbling on **grass**,
staring off **and** thinking about **nothing...**

How does it **feel**
to **be food?**

Thora thought and **thought.**
She wanted the vikings to understand.

sometimes it's hard to know what to say.

How can Thora get others to care about little snails?

I don't know the answer,
and neither does Thora.

At **seven** o'clock,
Aksel and **Krog** called
for **Thora** and the **tweeters**
to come **have** dinner.

The vikings had **made a beautiful** salad with **lots** and **lots** of **green** things, some chopped **red** onion, orange slices, and **almonds** on top.

(**Of course PLENTY of garlic**-onion-**beet**-spinach-**mango**-**carrot**-grapefruit **juice was also served**).

Thora almost cried at the **sight** of the **juice.**

She couldn't **stop** thinking about **those** poor **snails**.

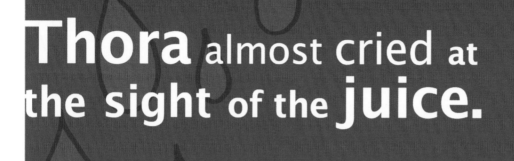

And then

she noticed there was
something **slimy** on her **foot.**

It felt

wiggly and **warm**

and **rather** *sluggish.*

Thora peeked under the table,
and this is what she saw:

All of the **yellow spotted snails**
were dancing gleefully, *and they were drinking*

garlic-
onion- **beet-** spinach- **mango-** carrot-

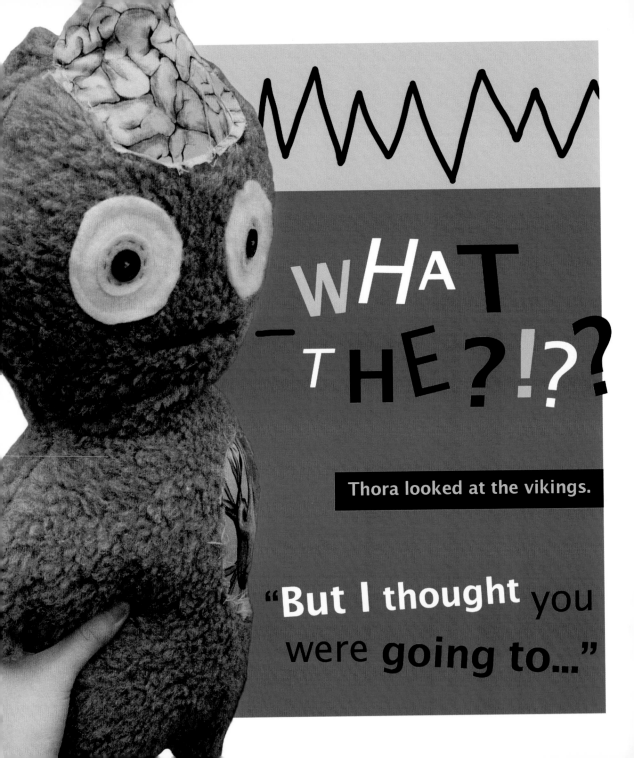

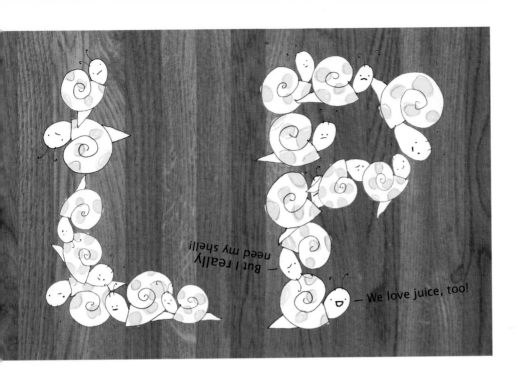

Thora was thrilled!

She just watched

as the snails rejoiced.

The yellow spotted snails looked

SO HAPPY

drinking their

garlic- **Onion**- beet- sp**inach**-
ma**n**go. **carrot**- grap**ef**ruit **juice**,

that...

the vikings got

TOT

ALLY

TOTA

ALLY

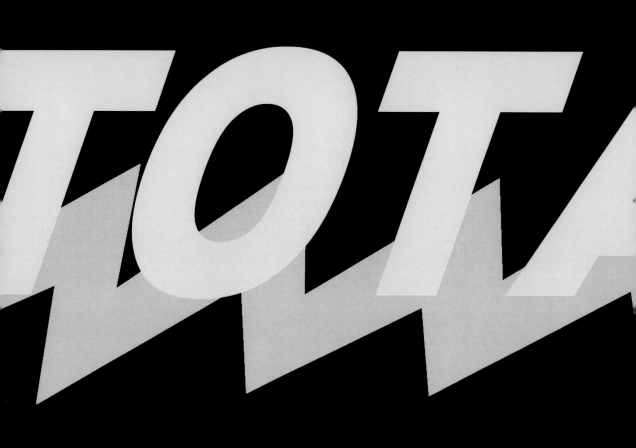

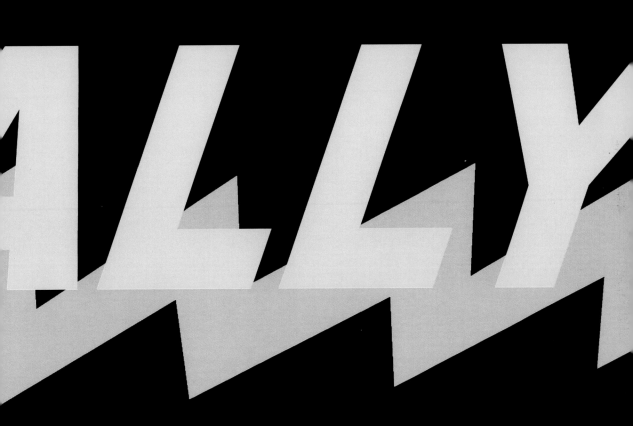